9/17

ARTURO AND THE BIENVENIDO FEAST

Anne Broyles   Illustrated by KE Lewis
Translated by Maru Cortes

PELICAN PUBLISHING COMPANY

GRETNA 2017

*The word "Pelican" and the depiction of a pelican are
trademarks of Pelican Publishing Company, Inc., and are
registered in the U.S. Patent and Trademark Office.*

ISBN 9781455622832
E-book ISBN 9781455622849

Printed in Korea
Published by Pelican Publishing Company, Inc.
1000 Burmaster Street, Gretna, Louisiana 70053

For Nico and Natalia, Garrett and Sara,
Aurora and Elías, Gwen, Callum, and Isla

Arturo stole a glance at his grandmother as he popped a handful of shredded cheese into his mouth.

Arturo le echó una miradita a su abuela mientras se metía un bocado de queso rallado a la boca.

"Leave some for the *pupusas*." Abue Rosa threw the dough into the mixing bowl—*thwack!*—and massaged the *masa* into a smooth ball.

"*Deja un poco para las pupusas.*" Abue Rosa aventó la masa al tazón—¡zas!—masajeando la masa hasta formar una bola suave.

Arturo mushed cheese and beans between his fingers to make the *pupusa* filling. When the *masa* was ready, Abue rolled small pieces into balls. Arturo added the cheese and bean mixture and pinched the dough shut, then flattened it between his palms.

Arturo presionó el queso y los frijoles entre sus dedos para hacer el relleno de las pupusas. Cuando la masa estaba lista, Abue amasó la masa formando pequeñas bolitas en círculos. Arturo agregó la mezcla de queso y frijol y apretó la masa para sellarla, después la aplanó entre las palmas de sus manos.

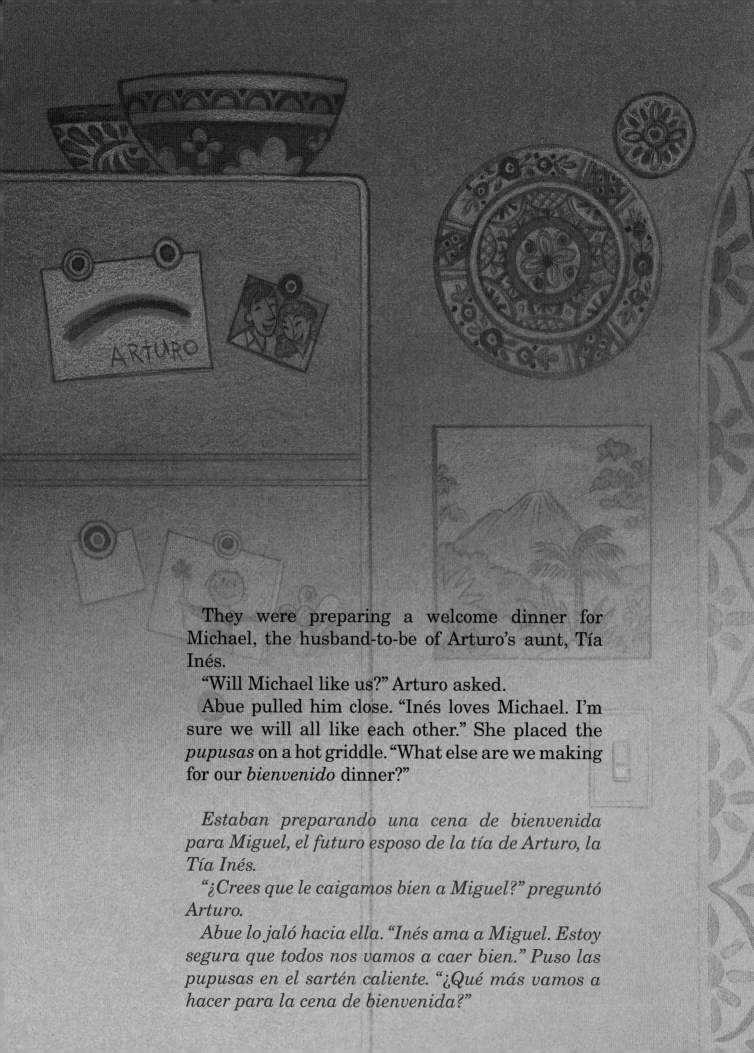

They were preparing a welcome dinner for Michael, the husband-to-be of Arturo's aunt, Tía Inés.

"Will Michael like us?" Arturo asked.

Abue pulled him close. "Inés loves Michael. I'm sure we will all like each other." She placed the *pupusas* on a hot griddle. "What else are we making for our *bienvenido* dinner?"

Estaban preparando una cena de bienvenida para Miguel, el futuro esposo de la tía de Arturo, la Tía Inés.

"¿Crees que le caigamos bien a Miguel?" preguntó Arturo.

Abue lo jaló hacia ella. "Inés ama a Miguel. Estoy segura que todos nos vamos a caer bien." Puso las pupusas en el sartén caliente. "¿Qué más vamos a hacer para la cena de bienvenida?"

Arturo jumped up and reached for paper and markers. "I'll make a menu!" FRIED PUPUSAS, he wrote. As the dough sizzled on the griddle, his mouth watered at the thought of biting into the cheesy, bean-filled treat.

Arturo se levantó y tomó una hoja de papel y los marcadores. "¡Voy a hacer un menú!" PUPUSAS FRITAS, escribió. Mientras la masa crujía en el sartén, se le hizo agua la boca pensando en morder el manjar relleno de quesito con frijolitos.

"And fried plantains," Abue said. "Inés loves *plátanos fritos* more than anything."

"Not more than she loves us," Arturo said, adding FRIED PLANTANES to the menu.

"Y plátanos fritos," dijo Abue. "Inés ama los plátanos fritos más que nada."

"No los ama más que a nosotros," dijo Arturo, agregando PLÁTANOS FRITOS al menú.

Abue Rosa laughed. "Your *tía* Inés certainly loves us—and Michael—more than she loves plantains! And we're serving *pollo*?"

Arturo nodded and added CHIKN. He poised his marker over the paper. "And salad?"

"*Sí. Curtido* and fruit salad."

Arturo wrote SLAW instead of CURTIDO, which was harder to spell. He took a bag of chopped cabbage from the refrigerator and waited for Abue to make the dressing.

"And chocolate-almond cake?" Arturo loved chocolate-almond cake as much as Tía Inés loved fried plantains.

"*Pastel* will be the perfect dessert."

Arturo added this to their list.

Abue turned off the griddle. "I'll warm the *pupusas* just before we eat."

Abue Rosa se rio. "¡Por supuesto que tu tía Inés nos ama—y a Miguel—más que a los plátanos machos! ¿Y vamos a servir pollo?"

Arturo asintió y agregó POLLO. Equilibró su marcador sobre el papel. "¿Y ensalada?"

"Sí. Curtido de col y ensalada de fruta."

Arturo escribió SLAW en vez de CURTIDO, pues fue más difícil para deletrear. Tomó una bolsa de col picada del refrigerador y esperó a Abue para hacer el aderezo.

"¿También pastel de chocolate con almendras?" A Arturo le encanta tanto el pastel de chocolate con almendras como a la Tía Inés le encantan los plátanos fritos.

"Pastel será el postre perfecto."

Arturo agregó esto a su lista.

Abue apagó la estufa. "Calentaré las pupusas justo antes de comer."

The day's bright sunshine filled the kitchen. Abue Rosa shielded her eyes and rubbed her forehead with her fingers. "*Me duele la cabeza.* A headache when we have so much to do!"

"Why don't you rest, Abue?"

"*Gracias, m'ijo.* I will." She lay down on the living-room couch. "Call me in a few minutes and I will finish cooking."

El brillo del amanecer alumbró la cocina. Abue Rosa cubrió sus ojos y se frotó la frente con sus dedos. "Me duele la cabeza. ¡El dolor de cabeza cuando tenemos tanto que hacer!"

"Por qué no descansas, Abue?"

"Gracias, m'ijo. Lo haré." Ella se echó en el sillón de la sala. "Llámame en pocos minutos y terminaré de cocinar."

Arturo created special paper placemats. He drew a rainbow for Abue, a cat for Tía Inés, and trucks for himself. What would Michael like?

Arturo hizo mantelitos especiales. Dibujó un arcoíris para Abue, un gato para la Tía Inés, y camioncitos para él. ¿Qué le gustaría a Miguel?

Arturo arranged the placemats on the table and carefully carried over plates, glasses, and silverware. "Abue? Which side does the fork—?"
She didn't stir.

Arturo organizó los mantelitos en la mesa y con mucho cuidado llevó los platos, los vasos, y los cubiertos. "¿Abue? ¿Pongo el tenedor del lado—?"
Ella no se despertó.

Arturo balanced a knife, fork, and spoon on each plate and decorated the table with candles. He pulled a stool up to the kitchen sink and washed grapes as Abue gently snored.

Arturo equilibró un cuchillo, tenedor, y cuchara en cada plato y decoró la mesa con velas. Jaló un banquito hacia el fregadero de la cocina y lavó las uvas mientras Abue roncaba dulcemente.

Arturo pictured thick brown frosting on chocolate-almond cake. "Abue? How do you make—?"

Arturo tiptoed into the living room and looked at his grandmother's peaceful face. He didn't want to wake her, so he would make the meal as best he could.

Arturo se imaginaba el denso glaseado sobre el pastel de chocolate con almendras. "Abue? ¿Cómo se hace—?"

Arturo entro de puntitas a la sala y miró la cara llena de paz de su abuela. No la quería despertar, haré la comida lo mejor que pueda.

The spoon clanked against the bowl as he mixed
bags of chocolate chips and almonds.

*La cuchara sonaba "clonch" contra el platón
mientras mezclaba las bolsas de chispas de
chocolate y almendras.*

Arturo often helped Abue make *plátanos fritos*. Now he peeled each plantain, used his fingers to squish each one into pieces, and left them on a plate for Abue Rosa to fry. As he scooped sugar from the canister and shook cinnamon into a bowl, the air filled with the powdery sweetness that would later coat the warm *plátanos*.

Arturo cada rato ayudaba a Abue a hacer plátanos fritos. Pelaba cada plátano, usó sus dedos para aplastar cada uno de ellos en pedazos y los dejó en la charola para que Abue Rosa los friera más tarde. Mientras sacaba el azúcar de un bote, espolvoreó la canela en un platón, el aire se llenó de polvo endulzado que más tarde cubriría los plátanos fritos.

The doorbell rang. Arturo touched Abue's shoulder. "They're here."

"Oh, no!" She sat up and smoothed her dress.

El timbré sonó. Arturo tocó el hombro de Abue. "Ya llegaron."

Ella se incorporó y alisó su vestido.

With hugs and kisses, Tía Inés entered and introduced Michael. Abue took his hands. "I'm sorry, but our dinner—"

"Come and see!" Arturo led the others into the dining room.

Con abrazos y besos, la Tía Inés entró y presentó a Miguel. Abue tomó sus manos. "Lo siento, pero nuestra comida—"

"¡Vengan y vean!" Arturó guió a los otros al comedor.

"*¡Bienvenidos!*"

"Wow!" Michael said. "What a feast. I'm going to like being part of this family!"

"¡Guau!" dijo Miguel. "Qué banquete. ¡Me va a encantar ser parte de esta familia!"

CURTIDO (Slaw)

½ head cabbage, shredded
1 large carrot, peeled and grated
½ medium yellow onion, thinly sliced
½ cup apple-cider vinegar
¼ cup water
½ teaspoon salt
½ teaspoon brown sugar
1 teaspoon dried oregano
½ to 1 teaspoon crushed red pepper flakes

Mix the vegetables in a large bowl. In a separate bowl, mix the remaining ingredients. Pour this dressing over the vegetables and stir. Cover and refrigerate for at least 2 hours. Makes about 4 cups.

PUPUSAS

For the dough:
2 cups masa harina
Pinch of salt
1½ cups warm water

For the filling:
1 cup grated cheese (quesillo, queso fresco, Monterey Jack, or mozzarella)
1 can refried beans
Vegetable oil
Salt

To make the dough: Combine the ingredients in a mixing bowl. Knead to form a smooth, moist dough like Play-Doh. If the mixture is too dry, add more water, 1 teaspoon at a time. If it is too sticky, add more masa harina. Cover the bowl with a clean towel and let stand for 10 minutes.

To make the filling: Mix the cheese and beans with a little oil and salt.

To make the *pupusas:* With lightly oiled hands, form the dough into 8 balls about 2 inches wide. Push your fingers into one of the balls, forming a small cup. Fill the cup with 1 tablespoon of filling, then wrap the dough around the filling to seal it. Making sure that the filling does not leak out, pat the dough back and forth between your hands to form a disk about ¼ inch thick. Repeat with the remaining balls.

To cook the *pupusas:* Heat a lightly oiled skillet over medium-high heat. Cook the *pupusas* for 2 to 3 minutes on each side until golden brown. Serve while still warm, with *curtido* on the side.

Glossary

Abue (*OB-way*): nickname for grandmother
Arturo (*ar-TOO-ro*): Arthur
bienvenido (*byen-veh-NEE-doh*): welcome
gracias (*GRAH-see-ahs*): thank you
Inés (*ee-NES*): a woman's name
masa (*MAH-sah*): dough made from hominy (corn)
me duele la cabeza (*may DWEL-ay lah cah-BAY-zah*): my head hurts
m'ijo (*MEE-ho*): my dear, sweetie
pastel (*pah-STEL*): cake
plantain (*PLAN-tin*): a fruit similar to a banana
plátanos fritos (*PLAH-tah-nohs FREE-tohs*): fried plantains
pollo (*POY-yoh*): chicken
pupusas (*poo-POO-sahz*): fried dough filled with beans, cheese, meat, etc.
sí (*see*): yes
tía (*TEE-ah*): aunt

Author's Note

Food is one of the ways families share love. Baking bread, cooking pasta, or making cookies with someone you love gives time together and something delicious to eat. When I was a little girl, my grandmother taught me how to make Peanut Butter Goop. It wasn't much of a recipe, really, just peanut butter, butter, and corn syrup, but I loved that we made it together to spread on toast. If my grandmother had come from Poland, we might have made *pierogis* (stuffed dumplings). If she had been from Korea, I might have learned how to make *kimchi* (fermented vegetables), or if her background was Ethiopian, we might have made *wat* (stew).

Abue and Arturo's menu includes foods from Latin America (Mexico, Central, and South America). How they work together, how Arturo cares for his *abuela* (grandmother), and how they welcome new family member Michael show the love they share.